THE GOLDEN COMPASS™

PAN

and the

Prisoners of Bolvangar

NEW LINE CINEMA
A Time Warner Company

SCHOLASTIC INC.
New York Toronto London Auckland Sydney
Mexico City New Delhi Hong Kong Buenos Aires

ISBN-13: 978-0-545-05933-6
ISBN-10: 0-545-05933-X

12 11 10 9 8 7 6 5 4 3 2 1   8 9 10 11 12 13/0

Printed in the U.S.A.   01

This printing, February 2008

CHAPTER ONE

*T*he Samoyed trapper's sledge hurtled on and on through the icy-cold night. Teams of howling dogs pulled hard, dragging the wooden vehicle across the snow as if they would never stop. It had been a good evening for the merciless Samoyed – his kidnapping plan had worked like a dream. Helpless on the back of the sledge, his captives could only hold on tight as the sledge raced across the icy terrain.

Pantalaimon, or Pan for short, huddled closer to his human, a twelve-year-old girl called Lyra. He was a dæmon – a special part of Lyra's soul that existed outside of her body in animal form. The pair of them had been in some pretty hair-raising situations before now – back in their hometown of Oxford, they were in trouble *all* the time. But this was different – they were in the freezing Arctic, and they'd been kidnapped.

It had all happened so quickly. They had set up camp with their allies, the Gyptians – a race of water travellers that roamed canals and rivers. The Gyptians were on a quest to rescue children who'd been snatched away by the Gobblers, wicked people led by the mysterious Mrs Coulter. Their mission had led them far north to the frozen polar wastes, where they believed the Gobblers had taken the children. Suddenly, the Gyptian's makeshift camp had been attacked by Samoyed raiders – hunters and marauders who were native to the region. In the confusion, Lyra and Pantalaimon had been grabbed by a raider and bundled on to the sledge, which had then hurtled away from the camp at high speed.

Lyra whispered comforting thoughts in Pantalaimon's ear. Everything would be all right. They would escape and find their way back to the Gyptians. And then they would continue with their quest to find the kidnapped children. Lyra reassured him that, in a day or two, this would all seem like a grand adventure.

Pantalaimon wasn't so sure. He licked his white fur over and over in an effort to remain calm. Right now, he was an ermine, but as Lyra's dæmon, he could change from cat to butterfly to frog to ... well, to any animal he chose. This wonderful ability would last until Lyra grew up. Once she was an adult, he would keep the same form – for ever. And neither he nor Lyra was yet sure what that shape would be.

Lyra nudged him urgently and the little dæmon looked up to see an eerie glow on the horizon. They were heading straight towards it. Pantalaimon shivered. He had a very bad feeling about all of this.

After a few moments, the sledge swooshed between two rows of poles that supported bright, powerful lights. They cast an unhealthy, yellow hue on the ice.

The sledge glided along the avenue of lamps and through a metal gate into a wide, open

space. It was perfectly flat and smooth and white, and measured about a hundred metres across. Around the edge of the space ran an impossibly high metal fence. Pantalaimon gazed round in awe. This must be Bolvangar – the place he'd heard mentioned in whispered tones. Whoever owned the place clearly didn't expect the inhabitants to escape. Not that there was much point in escaping from somewhere that was slap bang in the middle of a frozen wasteland anyway.

At last, the sledge slid to a halt at the far end of the open space. They were in front of a cluster of low, white buildings connected by tunnels humped under the snow. At one end of the buildings was a stout metal mast that stretched twenty metres into the sky.

Roughly, the Samoyed cut Lyra loose from her bonds and hauled her to her feet. Then she and her dæmon were dazzled by a powerful lamp, which shone at them from the door of the building. A figure in a coal-silk anorak was silhouetted against the light, his features impossible to make out.

They'd arrived.

CHAPTER TWO

*W*ith a squeak of fear, Pantalaimon became a mouse and scurried into Lyra's hood, where he crouched, trembling. After a brief exchange with their captor in a foreign tongue, the other man stepped forward. To their surprise, he was not a Samoyed. When the man spoke to them, it was in perfect English.

'Does your dæmon always take that form?' he asked Lyra curiously. 'Has it settled?'

Without thinking, Pantalaimon gave the interrogator the answer he sought. The little dæmon turned into a stoat and hissed angrily.

'Very good,' said the man. He reached into his purse and pulled out several heavy coins, which he gave to Lyra's abductor. Samoyeds were hunters by nature, but kidnapping was far more profitable – the people at Bolvangar paid well for children. The thug returned to his sledge and flicked his whip at the panting dogs. In an instant, he was gone, speeding out of the compound towards the outside world – and freedom.

Lyra and Pantalaimon were trapped.

'You'd better come in,' said the official, not unpleasantly. 'It's warm and comfortable inside. What's your name?'

'He doesn't know who we are!' Pantalaimon hissed to Lyra.

Lyra stepped into a small entrance hall. It was immaculate – white and steel, shining and spotlessly clean. 'Lizzie,' she boldly introduced herself. 'Lizzie Brooks.'

Pantalaimon approved wholeheartedly of this lie. After all, if these people didn't know who they were – why tell them?

'That's a lovely name,' said the official vaguely, as if his mind were on other, more important matters.

'What is this place?' asked Lyra.

'You'll like it,' replied the man. 'It's called the Experimental Station.'

Pantalaimon gulped. This definitely didn't sound good. Together, he and Lyra followed the official down a corridor every bit as antiseptic as the entrance hall they'd just left. Flashes of activity sounded through the doors that they passed – enough to give them tantalizing clues as to what was going on, but not enough to reveal anything worthwhile.

'What were you doing so far north, Lizzie?' asked the official. '*That* must be an interesting story.'

'He's trying to catch us out!' Pantalaimon warned his mistress.

But Lyra was ready. 'My dad and uncle, they took me north,' she said. 'They're traders.'

It was difficult to read the official's expression. 'Well, you're very lucky that those Samoyeds found you when you got lost,' he said at last, staring hard at Lyra.

'But, I wasn't lost,' she said. 'There was fighting—'

Pantalaimon thought back a few hours to what had actually happened. They had certainly not been lost. They had been kidnapped, like the poor Gyptian children they were searching for. He didn't trust this man, any more than he trusted Mrs Coulter. The charming and elegant woman had befriended Lyra and Pantalaimon, but her beautiful appearance masked a cruel and devious nature. Mrs Coulter's Golden Monkey dæmon had tried to steal Lyra's precious alethiometer – a remarkable truth-telling device. To their horror, they had also found out that Mrs Coulter was in fact the ruthless leader of the Gobblers.

The man strode on, dismissing Lyra's protests as if they were the ramblings of a confused child. 'Oh, I don't think so,' he said quickly. 'I think you must have wandered away from your father's party and got lost. Those huntsmen found you on your own and brought you straight here.' His words were calm and reasonable, as if he were trying to convince Lyra to agree with his version of events. 'That's what happened, Lizzie,' he said firmly. 'Often, in the intense cold, you fall asleep and have bad dreams and you can't remember what's true and what isn't. Your father is safe and sound ... and won't he be happy when he finds out that you're safe and sound too!' He beamed happily.

By now, they had arrived at a door that stood slightly open. From within came a low, menacing hum. There was something evil in that room – Pantalaimon knew it.

'What do you do here?' asked Lyra.

The doctor paused before replying. 'We help children grow up,' he said at last. His tone was pleasant, but the words were ominous.

In the distance, a bell began to ring, echoing through the dazzlingly white building.

The doctor checked his watch nervously. He suddenly seemed very agitated and anxious. 'Already?' he muttered to himself. It was clear something was worrying him. He took a deep breath and sighed, closing the

door behind him. 'I'm afraid we'll have to finish our chat later,' he said. 'I've got to welcome a special guest. You'd better run along to dinner now.' And with that, the strange conversation was at an end.

CHAPTER THREE

*I*t was certainly the most bizarre canteen Pantalaimon had ever seen. The room was large – decorated on three walls with bright, cheery colours. On the fourth wall was a blown-up photogram of a tropical island. There were thirty or so children here, all about Lyra's age or younger, and a sprinkling of adults. Everyone chattered noisily as they ate their meal.

As Lyra walked into the canteen, some of the girls she passed stopped talking. They stared at her curiously, but most of the others were far too busy eating to take any notice of the new arrival. Nurses were positioned here and there among the tables, presumably to keep order, but they seemed absorbed in their meals too.

Pantalaimon sensed that Lyra was trying to

keep a low profile while she checked everything out. He snuggled closer to her while he too scanned the room for clues and tried to work out what was going on. Were these the missing Gyptian children? Why would so many of them be kept in a strange, white prison in the middle of nowhere? And if it was called the Experimental Station, just what were the experiments? Questions tumbled through his mind as thick and fast as heavy snow.

Suddenly, Lyra froze. Pantalaimon followed her gaze … then he saw him too.

It was Roger – Lyra's best friend from Oxford and the boy whose mysterious disappearance was one of the reasons they had come all this way. When the Gobblers had first starting kidnapping children from Oxford, Lyra had promised Roger that if anything happened to him, she would find him and rescue him. And here he was… it didn't seem possible.

He was sitting at the far end of the room,

a little apart from everyone else. Then, as if feeling their eyes upon him, he looked up and a huge grin lit up his face. He sprang to his feet and pushed his chair back, ready to rush over to them. But Lyra gave the tiniest shake of her head, warning him to stay where he was. Roger immediately got the message and sank back into his seat again. He looked barely able to conceal his delight.

Pantalaimon could tell that Lyra was thrilled too. But she hid her feelings well. Lyra slowly made her way towards Roger, looking for all the world like the new girl nervously searching for an inconspicuous place to sit. Quickly, she slid into a seat at Roger's table.

'I knew,' muttered Roger under his breath. 'I knew you'd come.'

'I promised, didn't I?' whispered Lyra to her long-lost friend. She gripped his hand tightly, as Pantalaimon and Salcilia – Roger's dæmon – tenderly touched noses. 'Roger,' she continued, 'do you know what they do to the kids here?'

Roger's reply was terse. 'They say they're gonna help us, do this operation, right? And then they'll send us home, and we won't have to worry about Dust.'

It was that word again. Dust. The mere mention of it was enough to make Pantalaimon shiver with fear. As far as he knew, Dust was strange particles from space that seemed to gather around human beings. But Dust seemed to cause a lot of trouble, and now it looked like Dust had something to do with the kidnapping of the children by Mrs Coulter and the Gobblers.

Lyra leant in close so there was no danger of being overheard. 'Did they say what Dust *was*?' she asked.

'No,' said Roger, shaking his head. 'Only that it was bad, like a disease or something … and they was giving us the operation to keep it away. Like they was doin' us a favour. But I never believed 'em. Once they call a kid in for the operation, you never see them again, Lyra.'

Pantalaimon gulped.

But Lyra was not shaken by this information. When she spoke, her voice was confident. 'That's all right,' she said. 'We've come to rescue you – me and the Gyptians. Tell the kids to have their warm clothes ready.'

'Gyptians?' murmured Roger. These were not the sort of people they were friends with back in Oxford. 'How ... how could they ever—?'

'They're *coming*, Roger.'

Lyra was fiercely insistent and Roger knew not to argue.

'When?' he asked.

'That's what I need to find out,' she replied. 'But not here. I need to be alone somewhere.'

Pantalaimon knew at once that she intended to find out the answer from the alethiometer. It was a device that looked very much like a golden compass, but it was so much more than that. The alethiometer had been given to her by the Master of Jordan College, her former home in Oxford. It was old. Very old. And few were able to use it. But somehow, Lyra had the talent to decipher the alethiometer's cryptic symbols and gain the answer to any question she asked.

Quickly, and without pausing to ask questions, Roger led Lyra to a small dining room. It was formal, austere and very dusty, totally unlike the bright, shiny canteen.

'They hardly ever use this one,' he said, looking up and down the white corridor nervously. 'But be quick...'

Wordlessly, Lyra slipped inside the room. She pulled out a chair from the table and sat down gratefully. Pantalaimon felt her begin to relax her mind in preparation. He knew that she needed silence in order to be able to read the alethiometer properly – and here, at last, she had it.

'What does it say?' asked Pantalaimon. 'Are the Gyptians coming?'

Carefully, Lyra turned the alethiometer's dials until the three hands pointed to the correct symbols. Then she concentrated upon its face and waited for the fourth hand to settle on a symbol. This would reveal the alethiometer's answer.

But the fourth hand continued to swing round and round.

'It won't answer,' said Lyra shortly. 'It's almost as if … as if it's disappointed in me for asking.' She paused, adding, 'But there's something else. It says I mustn't let Mrs Coulter get hold of it, or we'll all die! But why would it—?'

A quiet tapping noise began to sound in the distance. It grew louder and louder, becoming the unmistakable click of heels, marching briskly towards them. There were other footsteps too. Whoever was approaching was not alone. The feet came to a halt, right outside the dining room.

Then a familiar voice spoke.

It was Mrs Coulter.

CHAPTER FOUR

*M*rs Coulter's clear voice pierced the air. 'I'm very interested in discovering just how several children wandered free from the Station,' she mused, her politeness masking an undercurrent of menace. As an agent for the Magisterium – the organization that governed people's lives – she now controlled the General Oblation Board, or G.O.B., which had authorized the abduction of the Bolvangar children. Her minions, the so-called 'Gobblers', brought their captives from far and wide to this final destination – the Experimental Station. Mrs Coulter was a powerful, dangerous enemy, and she did not tolerate failure.

Terrified, Pantalaimon and Lyra looked at each other and then around the sparsely furnished room. There was absolutely *nowhere* for them to hide.

Outside the room, Mrs Coulter's companion ignored her comment. 'Are you supposed to be here, boy?' he asked instead.

Obviously, they had discovered Roger.

'No, sir,' Lyra's friend muttered nervously.

'Then off with you,' was the curt response.

The door swung open and a group of people entered the formal dining room – Mrs Coulter, the official who had greeted Lyra and Pantalaimon, a doctor, an important-looking nurse and several workers. Each was accompanied by their dæmon. The new arrivals glanced around the empty room before seating themselves at the table.

'Mrs Coulter,' said the official, 'I hope you understand that the question is moot. Any child – severed or complete – who escaped from the facility would not last very long in the cold.'

'We have already recovered two of the three missing children,' the head nurse added quickly.

Lyra and Pantalaimon crouched beneath the table. Of all the many hiding places they'd ever used, this was probably the worst. At any moment, one of the party could bend to tie a shoelace, they would be discovered and then they would be in *real* trouble. After all, the last time they'd seen Mrs Coulter, Lyra had smashed her dæmon's paw. They'd heard the creature – a Golden Monkey – screaming in agony as they'd escaped over the rooftops of London.

Gentle scampering sounded through the wooden table. This was followed by an anxious chitter-chattering noise.

It was the Golden Monkey.

The scheming little creature sounded restless, as if he sensed something. Pantalaimon began to tremble uncontrollably. Not even Lyra's reassuring touch could calm him.

'Alive?' continued Mrs Coulter, talking of the two children who had been found.

There was no reply.

'That is unfortunate,' she said, not sounding particularly upset. 'We might have learned from them.'

Without warning, the head nurse's terrier dæmon peered under the table, his dark, beady eyes fixing immediately on the hidden twosome. The little dog exploded in a frenzy of barking, but Pantalaimon changed into a deadly snake, rearing up, ready to strike with his flickering tongue—

'Bobby!' scolded the nurse. 'Hush!'

The terrier's barks became whimpers and then he retreated out of sight.

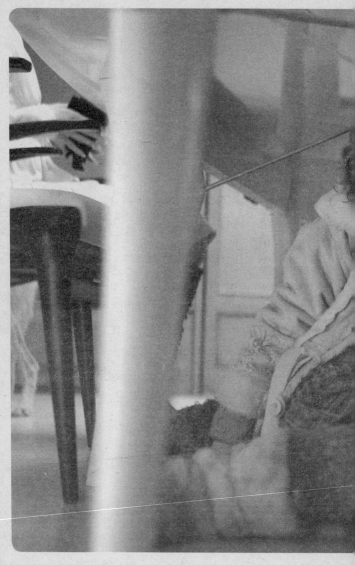

'Lyra!' whispered Pantalaimon, in utter amazement. 'She didn't listen to her dæmon!' This was *not* the way things worked. Humans and dæmons were connected by an invisible bond of energy, which enabled them to share each other's thoughts, feelings and sensations. They were part of each other; they listened to each other. They certainly didn't tell each other to be quiet.

More scrabbling from the tabletop interrupted Pantalaimon's anxious thoughts. The Monkey was on the move again. The sounds scurried nearer to the end of the table. Any moment now, Mrs Coulter's dæmon would poke its golden head into their hiding place and they would be discovered.

Closer and closer came the tiny paws...

CHAPTER FIVE

M rs Coulter, sounding suddenly tired, stifled a yawn. 'It's been a long journey. I think I'll go to bed.'

The Golden Monkey's scrambling paws stopped – and retreated.

Pantalaimon heaved a sigh of relief.

'Of course,' said the Bolvangar official politely. 'The orderlies will show you to your chambers.'

Mrs Coulter pushed back her chair and she rose gracefully from the table. And as she stood, so did everyone else. There were no clues for guessing who was in charge around here. As the door closed behind her, the tension in the air vanished instantly. Now, the atmosphere was relaxed, lighthearted almost.

'Wouldn't want to be on the wrong side of her, I can say that much,' the official said. 'She's positively ghoulish.' He paused before addressing the others again. 'Do you remember the first experiments, when she was so keen to see them pulled apart—?'

Pantalaimon felt an icy fear grip his heart. What did Mrs Coulter mean to pull apart, exactly? It was with the greatest difficulty that he remained silent. Lyra did not. She gasped out loud and gave such a shudder that she accidentally nudged a nearby table leg. It scraped noisily across the floor.

'What was that?' said the official at once.

The nurse had seen them. 'Down there!' she snapped.

'Quick!' ordered the doctor, pointing beneath the table to where Lyra and Pantalaimon tried unsuccessfully to remain hidden. The orderlies and other doctors dived towards them and

Lyra was unceremoniously dragged out, biting, scratching, kicking, punching and spitting in fury.

But Pantalaimon fared worse.

For the first time in the dæmon's life, another human dared to touch him. The doctor grabbed his fur and held him up high. And no matter how Pantalaimon struggled, he didn't let go. The dæmon shook uncontrollably, crying in pain and fear, currents of energy zipping and fizzing from his small body.

'You *can't*...' sobbed Lyra, hardly able to get the words out. 'Not *allowed* ... not *supposed* to touch...' And then, stunned beyond belief by Pantalaimon's shocking treatment, she fell silent.

'Who is she?' asked the head nurse.

'The new child,' replied the doctor. 'Lizzie something.'

The nurse thought for a moment. 'She can't return to the other children,' she decided. 'And Mrs Coulter—'

'No,' agreed the official. He knew at once what the nurse meant to say. 'She mustn't know. Certainly not.' He paused before making his decision. 'There's only one thing we can do, it seems to me,' he said.

The words struck icy terror into Pantalaimon's heart.

The official strode purposefully out of the dining room. An orderly followed him, carrying Lyra. She hung limply in his arms, all the fight gone out of her. The head nurse brought up the rear, Pantalaimon held tightly in her iron grip. Several doctors appeared, adding to the strange procession.

Down the bright, white corridor they went, the distant murmur of children growing fainter and fainter, while the wind howled eerily

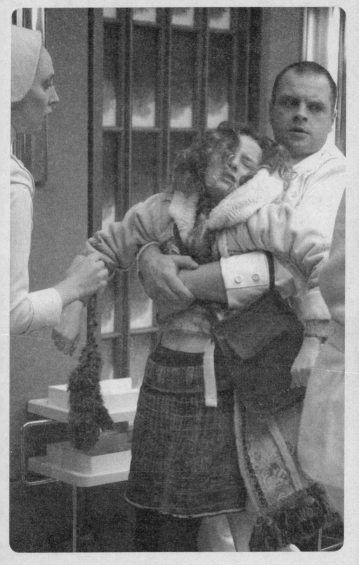

outside the Experimental Station. Soon, they reached a large, metal hatch secured with a locking wheel.

From beyond the hatch, there came the sound of a distant, but familiar hum – a low, throbbing that made ears ring and fingers buzz with its unseen power. Pantalaimon realized that it was the unnerving sound they'd heard when they first arrived at Bolvangar.

'Quickly now!' said the official urgently.

One of the doctors turned the wheel, which slid round smoothly as if it were oiled often. Majestically, the door hissed open. The doctors rushed through the gap, their feet clattering noisily on the hard floor in their haste.

The door shut behind them with a thud, eliminating all noise from the rest of the building.

Pantalaimon looked around. They were in

an operating theatre. It was a cold, clinical place filled with strange equipment. Was *this* where the mysterious experiments took place? In the centre was a large operating table – and on top a cage made of gold mesh. The little dæmon half expected to see a magnificent bird inside, but it was empty apart from a double thickness of more delicate mesh that divided the cage in two. Most terrifying of all was the huge, shiny guillotine that hung above the cage. Its blade shone wickedly.

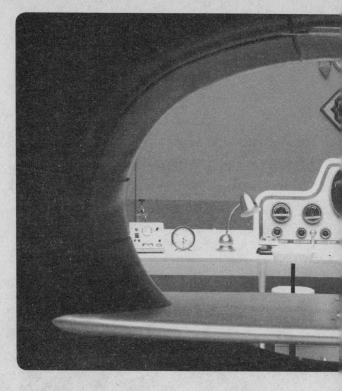

Lyra took one look at the guillotine and began to scream, long and loud.

Roughly, the orderly clamped a rough hand over her mouth to stifle the noise. 'What a palaver,' he muttered crossly to the others, who raised their eyebrows in agreement.

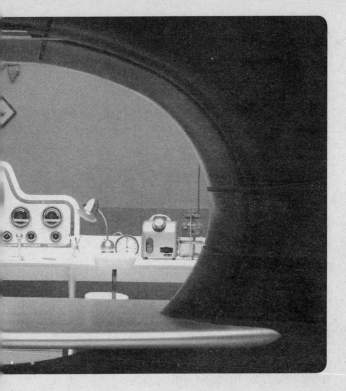

Lyra stretched her fingertips towards her beloved dæmon, who in turn reached for her. But even though they strained towards each other like two magnets, they were not allowed to touch. Instead, they were carefully set down in the golden cage – one either side of the fine mesh dividers.

'Don't fret, dear,' said the head nurse to Lyra. 'It's only a little cut.'

This sounded painful to Pantalaimon. A cut was a cut, whichever way he looked at it. And it was bound to hurt.

'You want to grow up, don't you?' asked the orderly. 'Well, this is how you grow up. All the adults get it.'

Lyra's dæmon found this hard to believe. Never in his entire life had he heard even a whisper about a mysterious procedure that made children grow up. As far as he knew, it just happened, like acorns turning into oak trees or night turning into day.

Lyra fought wildly against the hands that held her captive, thrashing her arms and legs in a vain attempt to free herself. But her hands were finally strapped against the operating table. She was trapped. She stared wide-eyed at Pantalaimon, who was imprisoned in the other cage, struggling against the head nurse.

'You'll never keep us apart!' cried Lyra to the group of orderlies, doctors and nurses. And then she spoke to Pantalaimon, as if reassuring him that whatever happened, nothing would change between them. 'Never, never, never...'

But the guillotine above them began to hum loudly as the machine that drove it whirred into motion. And somehow, the deadly instrument's power illuminated the threads of glowing energy that connected Lyra and Pantalaimon – the bond it was designed to cut forever.

Slowly, relentlessly, the guillotine began to descend.

CHAPTER SIX

*S*uddenly, a voice rang out, echoing around the room. 'What is going on here?'

Never had Pantalaimon thought he would be glad to hear that voice – cool and charming with an undercurrent of menace. It was Mrs Coulter.

The medical staff gathered in the operating theatre turned to see the head of Bolvangar Experimental Station and the leader of the Gobblers standing by the open door. She'd entered the room so quietly that none had seen her arrive. Guiltily, one of the doctors flipped a switch. The great machine whined to a halt and was silent once more.

Mrs Coulter approached the operating table. 'And who is this ch—?' She drew in her breath sharply as she recognized the girl strapped inside the cage. 'Lyra!' she cried.

Pantalaimon watched entranced as a succession of different emotions flashed across the woman's face. There was surprise, shock and finally anger.

It was all too much for Lyra. She took one look at the woman who had lured her away from Oxford with promises of travel and adventure, only to disappoint her with an attempt to steal her precious alethiometer – and passed out.

***

Pantalaimon nestled against Lyra in his cat-form, contented and relaxed. He never thought he'd get this close to Lyra again and he was so comfortable, so warm, so at home. It was where he belonged. He didn't even care that they were in Mrs Coulter's luxurious chambers. Being with his beloved Lyra was all that mattered.

Lyra slept. She was at peace, for the moment. Then she snapped awake with a gasp, crying out, 'They was going to cut … to cut—'

Mrs Coulter hushed her gently from her chair nearby. 'They won't ever do it to you,' she murmured. 'No one's going to harm you, Lyra, darling.'

Pantalaimon was confused. When they'd escaped from Mrs Coulter and her Golden Monkey, taking the alethiometer with them, the woman had been livid. He'd never seen anyone so angry. And now she was, well … nice. What had changed things? Why should she care what happened to Lyra and her dæmon? It was all very strange indeed.

'But Roger…' protested Lyra. 'And the other kids…'

'You don't have to go back with the other children,' said Mrs Coulter, smiling reassuringly. 'Not now I've got my little assistant back.

My favourite!'

None of this pretty speech appeared to convince Lyra that the woman had everyone's best interests at heart. 'But why do you do it to them?' she persisted. 'How can you be so cruel?'

'It may seem cruel, Lyra,' Mrs Coulter said patiently. 'But it's for their own good. Just a little cut ... and they're safe from Dust for ever.'

'I don't understand,' said Lyra.

Neither did Pantalaimon. All he knew was that this strange Dust – which adults kept going on and on about – seemed to cause a whole lot of problems. Just like the Golden Monkey. While Mrs Coulter had been speaking, the beady-eyed creature had blocked Pantalaimon's attempts to find a way out of the lavishly furnished room. Reluctantly, the little dæmon gave up and returned to Lyra.

'What's so bad about Dust?' Lyra went on.

'Dust is *evil itself*,' said Mrs Coulter, staring right at her. 'A long, long time ago, one of our ancestors made a terrible mistake. They defied the Authority. And at that moment, Dust came into the world. Ever since then, we've been *sick*. So sick we haven't even *known*. Sick with Dust.'

Pantalaimon gulped. He hadn't the foggiest idea what Mrs Coulter was talking about, but whatever it was sounded *bad*.

Mrs Coulter had paused to allow the words to sink in. And when she continued, she sounded happier, hopeful almost. 'But there is a way out,' she said. 'You see, Dust doesn't collect around innocent children … but just a little bit later, at what we call the age of puberty.'

This word sounded very familiar to Pantalaimon. He was pretty sure that puberty meant the time when a child grew up. And from Mrs Coulter's next words, it appeared that he was right.

'When your dæmon settles,' the elegant woman explained, 'the Dust swarms about you, trying to work its mischief. And it gets into you through your dæmon, and innocent children begin to have all sorts of nasty thoughts and feelings.'

Pantalaimon didn't like the sound of this at all. Not one bit. Suddenly, the dæmon seemed to be the bad character in this curious tale – and he wasn't used to being cast in that role.

However, Mrs Coulter had the solution. 'But all it takes to stop it from happening is a snip,' she said brightly. 'A tiny little snip. Your dæmon doesn't die – he's just not connected, like a special, special pet. All the nurses have had the operation and they seem happy, don't they?'

In a flash, the nurse's strange behaviour

became clear. Pantalaimon remembered how the woman had treated her terrier dæmon. She had snapped angrily at him, when the little creature had only been trying to tell her that Lyra and Pantalaimon were hiding under the table. She had ignored what the terrier had to say. This wasn't how a person spoke to their dæmon – not unless the dæmon was no longer a part of them...

While they'd been talking, the Golden Monkey had been scampering about, sniffing the air as if searching for something. Pantalaimon hoped that the alethiometer were safely hidden – it must be this that the devious-looking creature was after.

Now that the words had sunk in, Lyra had a question for Mrs Coulter. Her eyes narrowed suspiciously before she spoke. 'Then why didn't you let them do it to me?' she asked.

Mrs Coulter smiled. 'That's a very grown-up question, dear,' she said. But she appeared reluctant to answer.

'No it en't!' cried Lyra. 'Any kid would ask that. Cause you want to do it to Roger, and he's my friend. And you done it to Billy Costa, and he was no better than a ghost!'

Billy Costa was a small, lost boy that she and Pantalaimon had found when travelling towards Bolvangar. He'd had no dæmon at all. Pantalaimon felt terribly sad when he remembered the boy.

'But you're not some Gyptian urchin, or servant boy,' said Mrs Coulter patiently. 'You're...' She stopped.

'I'm what?' asked Lyra.

Her words hung in the air for what seemed like an age before the woman replied.

'You will find out sooner or later,' said Mrs Coulter at last. 'Lyra, your parents didn't die in an airship accident. Now, I will tell you the truth. Your parents were not married when you were born. And so they were separated. Your father was stripped of all his lands and his wealth. And your mother? Well, she was stripped of *you*.'

Lyra stared at her, as if not sure what to make of this. Pantalaimon was none the wiser. If Lyra was not an orphan, then who *were* her parents? Did this strange, contradictory woman know the answer?

But before Lyra could ask anything, Mrs Coulter continued. 'Now, I almost forgot,' she said briskly. 'I think the Master of Jordan gave you something, didn't he?'

Pantalaimon sighed to himself. Did this woman never give up? He suspected not. She had wanted the alethiometer before and she wanted it still. She looked like the sort of person who always got what she wanted.

'He gave you an alethiometer,' said Mrs Coulter sweetly. 'The trouble is, it wasn't his to give. He must have known that, since it took him *ever so long* to say who he'd given it *to*.'

This didn't sound good at all. What had Mrs Coulter done to the Master to drag the truth out of him? Lyra clutched her small leather satchel to her chest, unaware that she was showing the woman exactly where she kept the precious alethiometer.

Mrs Coulter's eyes followed the bag greedily. 'Ah, I see you have it,' she said, looking both thrilled and relieved. 'It really ought to be properly looked after. I can save you the trouble of carrying it around…' she offered. 'Really, it must have been such a puzzle, wondering what a silly old thing like that was any good for.'

Lyra stared right at Mrs Coulter for a few seconds and then her shoulders sagged in defeat. 'All right,' she said. 'Here it is.'

Appalled, Pantalaimon watched as Lyra reached into her bag. But it was not the alethiometer that she withdrew. Instead, Lyra pulled out a small, round metal tin. At a distance, it might be mistaken for the precious object Mrs Coulter sought. But this was something entirely different. Inside was the spy-fly – a clockwork creature running on evil energy that Mrs Coulter had sent to spy on Lyra and the Gyptians. Luckily, the Gyptians had captured it and now it was trapped inside the sealed tin Lyra was carrying. Furious at its imprisonment, the creature would attack anyone in its path if it escaped.

'What's this?' cooed Mrs Coulter, leaning forward to whisk the object from Lyra's hand. 'What a funny old tin! Did you put it in here to keep it safe, dear?'

Despite the seriousness of the situation, Pantalaimon found himself struggling to keep a straight face. Mrs Coulter thought that the alethiometer was hidden inside

the metal tin! She was going to get a very nasty surprise indeed if she managed to get the tin open.

It would serve her right, though, for trying to take Lyra's prized possession.

Slowly at first, and then with increasing urgency, the woman tried to open the tin, tugging at it, tearing with her fingernails until her patience wore thin. She reached into her belongings and produced a delicate little knife. This she used to prize it open. Unable to resist the lure of the alethiometer, the Golden Monkey slunk over to watch.

As the two halves of the tin were wrenched apart at last, a curious buzzing noise filled the room.

'That sound…' murmured Mrs Coulter, looking puzzled. She and her dæmon leaned closer to the tin, closer, closer until—

Crash!

Furious at being trapped for so long, the spy-fly had rocketed from its metal prison and smashed hard into the Golden Monkey's face. The Monkey screamed in agony, throwing himself violently backwards in an attempt to escape from the frenzied creature. He collided with Mrs Coulter who cried out in pain. The spy-fly – a blur of whirring, buzzing metal – attacked Mrs Coulter next, clawing at her long, elegant neck.

Lyra and Pantalaimon watched in awe, realizing that their captors were far too busy beating off the furious spy-fly to pay attention to a small girl and her dæmon.

'Run, Pan!' cried Lyra.

Pantalaimon didn't need to be told twice. He scampered out of the door, followed swiftly by Lyra. Together they ran down the long white corridor – away from Mrs Coulter and the Golden Monkey, away from the Gobblers, away from Bolvangar and towards freedom. Soon they would be safely back with their Gyptian friends – and they would free the captive children of Bolvangar.

GLOSSARY

The world of the Golden Compass is a world very much like ours, in a parallel universe. Much of it would be familiar to us – the continents, the oceans, Brytain, Norroway and the North Pole ... but much is shockingly different. On this parallel Earth, a person's soul lives on the outside of their body, in the form of a dæmon – a talking animal spirit that accompanies them through life. A child's dæmon can change shape, assuming all the forms that a child's infinite potential inspires; but as a person ages, their dæmon gradually settles into one form, according to their character and nature.

CHARACTERS

Lyra

Lyra Belacqua is a twelve-year-old girl who has been left by her Uncle Asriel to be raised by the scholars and fellows of Jordan College in Oxford, Brytain. Headstrong, rebellious, and wilful, Lyra's carefree existence comes to an end after numerous children, including her friend Roger, mysteriously begin to disappear. Lyra's dæmon is Pantalaimon (Pan).

Mrs Coulter

Strikingly glamorous – yet mysteriously sinister – Mrs Coulter is a beautiful, powerful woman who takes a particular interest in Lyra. Her mysterious aims are in some way tied in with Lyra's very fate. Mrs Coulter's dæmon is a nameless Golden Monkey.

Roger Parslow

The Jordan College kitchen boy who is Lyra's best friend and playmate. The more cautious of the two, Roger's abduction sets in motion a string of events that thrusts Lyra on a perilous journey to fulfil her destiny. Roger's dæmon is Salcilia.

Gyptians

A nomadic group of waterfarers who live on canal-boats, the Gyptians are the descendants of warriors and traders from the east. There are six Gyptian tribes, harking back to all corners of the globe. After fleeing from Mrs Coulter, Lyra is rescued by the Western tribe. She falls under the protection of John Faa – the leader of the Western Gyptians – and his chief adviser, Farder Coram. With many of their own children taken by the Gobblers, the six Gyptian tribes band together. Accompanied by Lyra, they voyage North to rescue the children – of every origin – abducted by the Gobblers.

The Gobblers

A sinister band of kidnappers who abduct the children of the poor and the marginalized – orphans, servant children, Gyptians – and take them North for unknown purposes.

DEFINITIONS

Alethiometer

Also known as the Golden Compass, the alethiometer is an extraordinarily intricate device that was made in the sixteenth century. Its needle seeks out, instead of true North, Truth itself. The ornamented face of the device is divided into 36 symbols, each of which may convey different meanings in combination with any of the others and according to the subtleties of the machine's motions. Reading the alethiometer is a difficult task, but Lyra Belacqua possesses a natural ability to use the instrument.

The Magisterium

The powerful organization that dominates the politics and society of Lyra's world, in Brytain and beyond. It has established a ruthless, iron-grip on the nations of the world.

There are worlds beyond our own
— the Compass will show the way ...

THE GOLDEN COMPASS™

Read all three books and follow the exciting
adventures of Pan, Iorek and the Golden Monkey!

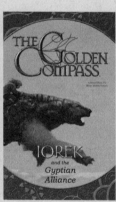

Pan and the
Prisoners of Bolvangar

Iorek and the
Gyptian Alliance

The Golden Monkey and the
Duel of the Dæmons